When We Grow Up

by Anne Rockwell

E. P. Dutton · New York

Copyright © 1981 by Anne Rockwell

Library of Congress Cataloging in Publication Data

Rockwell, Anne F.   When we grow up.

Summary: Pictures demonstrating the various jobs
children want to have when they grow up.
1. Occupations — Juvenile literature — Pictorial works.
[1. Occupations] I. Title
HF5381.2.R63   331.3'4   80-21768   ISBN 0-525-42575-6

Published in the United States by E. P. Dutton, A Division
of Elsevier-Dutton Publishing Company, Inc., New York

Published simultaneously in Canada by Clarke,
Irwin & Company Limited, Toronto and Vancouver

Editor: Ann Durell   Designer: Riki Levinson

Printed in the U.S.A.   First Edition
10 9 8 7 6 5 4 3 2 1

We go to school.
We learn to read, to write,
and to do arithmetic.
We are going to be smart people
when we grow up.

Elizabeth wants to be a photographer and take pictures for a newspaper.

Edmund wants to be a veterinarian
and make sick animals well.

Christine wants to be a clown
and make people laugh.

Emily wants to be an astronaut
and walk upon the moon.

Arthur wants to be a banker
and give people money,
because he is good at counting.

Amy wants to be a writer,
because she likes to read books.

Jim wants to be a carpenter
and build houses for people.

Louis wants to be
a construction worker
and build skyscrapers high in the sky.

Nancy wants to be a plumber
and fix water pipes when they leak.

Ned wants to be an artist
and paint pictures to hang in museums.

Milton wants to be a pilot
and make a big jet fly.

Martha wants to be a mechanic
and have her own gas station,
where people bring their cars.

Mark wants to be a barber
and cut people's hair.

What about me?
I want to be a teacher
like Mr. Raymond,
because he is so nice.

What will you be
when you grow up?

ANNE ROCKWELL wanted to be many things when she grew up, including a telephone lineman (because they can see so far), an archaeologist, and a comic strip writer. She wrote this book because she believes "all children have secret dreams about what they want to be when they grow up, but they are rarely asked about them. I wanted to get them talking about their ambitions. I also wanted to write a book emphasizing contemporary careers."

Mrs. Rockwell is the author and illustrator of many books, including *I Like the Library* and *Willy Runs Away*. She lives in Old Greenwich, Connecticut.